A new SCARETOWN book is released every month.
Sign up to the mailing list at
www.scaretownbooks.com for access to exclusive
deals on the newest releases.

Join the conversation at
www.twitter.com/scaretownbooks

ISBN: 9798683029647

WWW.SCARETOWNBOOKS.COM

For Olivia and Henry.

THE TEACHER ATE MY HOMEWORK

L.A. Drake

CHAPTER ONE

"SLOW DOWN, JACK!"

I paused. My sister, Ellie, was jogging to catch up. Her blonde hair flopped and flailed around her shoulders as she made her way up the sleepy suburban path towards me.

"Don't leave me behind, Jack, I don't want to walk in on my own."

It was our first day at our new school. Our dad had been transferred to a new job with the government on the Friday and we had upped-sticks, moved house and left our friends behind by Monday. The school gates were large and imposing. Intricate and ornate metalwork adorned them from top to bottom.

As we entered school property, the small trickle of other kids around us turned into a torrent and soon we were being jostled on all sides as boys and girls in black blazers made their way to class. I turned to see a tuft of blonde hair disappear into the mass of bodies.

"Ellie!" I shouted.

A small, thin hand burst through a gap in the throng. I grabbed it and pulled.

"So many kids!" Ellie said, brushing a mess of hair from her smiling face.

"Come on," I said. "We have to report to reception for our induction."

Ellie spotted a sign and we made our way across the schoolyard and through a small red door. The reception area couldn't have been more different from the mayhem outside. There were half a dozen comfy looking chairs in a circle around a coffee table laden with magazines. Gentle music lapped at our ears and the scent of freshly picked flowers greeted our nostrils. At the far end of the room was the smiling face of a friendly-looking receptionist.

"Hello, there! You must be the Fergusons! We've been expecting you," the lady said, her smile stretching even wider than when we entered.

"Jack, I presume?" she said, offering Ellie an outstretched hand. "I'm just kidding. Ellie, right?" Ellie looked at her and frowned. I smiled. Ellie's grumpy face never fails to amuse me.

"Hi, we're here for the induction," I said, puncturing the awkward silence.

"Ah, yes, about that," she replied, her smile faltering. "We're a bit busy this morning so you'll have to make do with an abridged tour by our very own handyman, Mr Michaels."

She gestured to our right and there, standing with his arms crossed next to a mop and bucket, was a gnarly looking man with wild grey hair down to his shoulders and the thickest eyebrows I'd ever seen.

"Right you are, kids, this way. Follow me! No dawdling now, let's get going!" he said with a grin somewhere between pain and pleasure stretched across his pockmarked face. Ellie and I both looked back to the receptionist for a way out of the situation but she ushered us forward without another word.

As we left the reception area, Mr Michaels forged ahead. He led us through the school so quickly that we both struggled to keep up. Ellie's backpack kept slipping off her shoulders so I carried it for her. Eventually, Mr Michaels stopped and leant against a locker. He looked at me, then at Ellie, then back at me. His eyes narrowed. He seemed confused.

"What did you say your name was? Fartison?" he said, straight-faced.

"Ferguson! Ellie and Jack Ferguson!" Ellie replied before I had the chance.

Mr Michaels paused for a second, looked us up and down one more time, then took off again. He power-walked through the various corridors, occasionally mumbling some information about each one without breaking stride. As we reached another hallway lined with doors, he stopped again.

"Do you like dogs?" he said, turning to face us.

"Dogs? Sure, I guess," I replied, struggling to catch my breath.

My answer seemed to please him as a wry smile emerged on his face and he bent down low until the smell of his breath was unavoidable.

"Then you're gonna love it here," he said with a wink.

Before we had a chance to think about what he meant, Mr Michaels leant on the handle behind him and swung open the big, black door.

CHAPTER TWO

"YOU," MR MICHAELS said, nodding in my direction, "in here. Little one, next door."

Ellie looked at me with wide eyes and a furrowed brow. I gave her a sympathetic smile and turned to enter the classroom. The door slammed shut as I looked up to see thirty sets of eyes staring back at me. At the front of the class was a tall man dressed all in black. His hair was short but shaggy and his blue eyes shone in bright contrast to his attire.

"Come in, Mr Ferguson. I'm Mr Cruft. We've been expecting you," he said calmly, barely looking up from the textbook he was reading.

I shuffled forward and clumsily eased myself down onto a lone empty chair. The sound of chair-leg screeching on concrete pierced the otherwise eery silence of the room. Once I was positioned, Mr Cruft continued reading aloud from where he had left off as if no time had passed. I unzipped my bag and placed my pencil case and books on the table as quietly as possible. I hoped Ellie's class was more welcoming.

Eventually, Mr Cruft stopped talking and assigned us work to be getting on with and the class burst into life. The silence I was greeted with erupted into the chaotic chatter of a dozen different conversations occurring at the same time. My personal silence, however, was undisturbed as I sat by myself pretending to be more comfortable than I felt.

After a while, I looked up to see a girl staring at me from across the room. Her hair was dark and almost completely covered her face. Like me, she was sat by herself. The other kids seemed to be staying a safe distance from her. Our eyes met and I instantly looked away, hoping she hadn't noticed. However, a few seconds later, a person-sized shadow was cast over my desk.

"Why were you looking at me?" the girl with the dark hair said.

"I wasn't! …I mean, I was but I didn't mean to. I was just looking around," I said. I could feel my cheeks starting to burn.

"You're new here," she said, more statement than question. "I'm Zaza."

"Hi, Zaza. I'm Jack," I replied, not sure whether she wanted to know. Zaza sat down next to me without another word. I looked around, expecting her to speak but she didn't.

"Is it a good school?" I asked, searching for something, anything, to fill the silence.

Zaza laughed and looked at me quizzically.

"It's fine if you know where to go. Or should I say, *when* to go."

I didn't know what she meant, but I decided not to question it. Soon enough, the teacher stood up again and the noise abated instantly. Zaza skulked off to her previous seat and remained there for the rest of the lesson.

The bell rang out loudly and I started to gather my things to leave. However, as I looked around, I noticed no one else had moved. Instead, they all sat and watched Mr Cruft patiently who, in turn, looked back at them in a strange kind of staring competition. Finally, Mr Cruft, with the tiniest nod of the head, indicated his approval and the students burst into life gathering their belongings.

The class squeezed themselves out the door in a homogenous mass of bodies, leaving me alone in the room with Mr Cruft. I stood up and made my way to the exit but, before I reached the door, Mr Cruft called my name. I took a step closer to his desk.

"Yes, sir?"

"First day at a new school. Very daunting, I'm sure," he said, still flicking through his textbook.

"Yes, I suppose so," I replied.

"Word of advice, Ferguson." He put the book down and looked me straight in the eyes for the first time. "When the final bell rings this afternoon, go home. Don't dawdle and don't linger with that sister of yours. Just go."

I wish I had listened.

CHAPTER THREE

THE REST OF the morning went by quickly and soon the bell rang for lunch. As all the other kids ran down the hallways and spilt out into the grounds, I once again lingered behind. Suddenly, I heard a voice call out and I turned to see Ellie running towards me. Her oversized backpack bounced high above her shoulders with every step.

"How was it?" I asked in earnest.

"So boring!" she replied with a grunt. "And the kids here are so…" She paused as we looked up to see Zaza between us and the outside. "…weird."

"Zaza, this is my sister Ellie," I said, with a feigned smile. "Ellie, this is Zaza, she's in my English class."

Zaza nodded and turned towards the exit. I thought for a hopeful second that she was going to leave without us but she turned and gestured for us to follow. Ellie looked at me. I shrugged and we both followed Zaza through the doors.

We turned a corner and found a low wall away from the other kids.

"Did you move here from the city?" Zaza said, sitting on the wall and taking sandwiches from her bag.

"Yes, we left on Friday," I said.

"And I suppose you think we're stupid?" Zaza said, looking me dead in the eyes.

"I'm... sorry? What? No. Why would we think that?" I said, stumbling over my words.

"All the city kids think we're stupid because we're from a small town. Because we don't have big buildings and shining lights."

"We don't think you're stupid!" Ellie said, pleadingly, but Zaza wasn't listening.

"Because it's a quiet town, a boring town, a *weird* town.' Ellie felt herself blushing as Zaza's diatribe continued. "But maybe they're right. Maybe we are weird. Would that be so bad?" She paused and waited for an answer.

"Oh, erm, no, of course not. Weird is good. We like weird," I said, frantically trying to find the right words.

"Maybe they're right to think we're strange, maybe they *should* be worried," Ellie and I exchanged glances. We both wanted the conversation to end, but Zaza persisted.

"I'll tell you what," she said, leaning in closer. "There *are* things you should be worried about in this school. Real things. Scary things." Her eyes were wide and frightening. Ellie let out a nervous giggle but Zaza's expression didn't change. "I've seen them. Beasts. Walking the halls after all the kids leave. They'll tear you limb from limb if you get too close," Zaza said, her voice barely a whisper.

I'd heard enough. We'd listened to the ramblings of a crazy person for too long and it was time we left. I made an excuse about having forgotten something in my last class. Ellie followed my lead without prompting and we left Zaza sitting on that low wall with a wild-eyed look still splashed across her pale, unflinching face.

As the doors shut behind us and we were safely out of sight, Ellie and I looked at each other and burst into laughter. A mixture of relief and confusion was written across our faces. A few moments later, we finally composed ourselves before realising we couldn't go back the way we came without bumping into Zaza. The only way back outside was to continue through the maze of hallways in an attempt to find another exit.

Neither of us knew the way so we wandered aimlessly through the corridors of our new school. Our footsteps echoed around the empty hallways and our voices seemed unnaturally loud in the otherwise eery silence.

Nevertheless, we were having fun talking and telling jokes until, suddenly, I saw a shadowy figure out the corner of my eye and screamed in terror.

CHAPTER FOUR

THE DARK FIGURE turned the corner and I saw a large set of pointed teeth gleaming out of the darkness. The beast fixed us in its steely gaze and paused for a second before leaping forward with a ferocious growl. I jumped in front of Ellie and tried to shield my face but the impact never came. Instead, there was a sharp, high-pitched sound that stopped the animal in its tracks.

I opened my eyes again and realised I was staring into the friendly face of a Labrador Retriever. Its large, pink tongue flopped out the side of its mouth. My cheeks flushed red as the affable hound bounded up to us. Ellie looked at me and laughed.

"It's just a dog, silly," she said, bending down to greet the animal.

"I knew that!" I replied, mopping the sweat from my forehead.

A few seconds passed as we fussed the dog before the sound of human footsteps made us stop. We looked up to see the caretaker, Mr Michaels, coming round the same corner as the Labrador had moments previously. He had a shiny silver whistle hanging from a string around his neck.

"Get your hands off my dog!" he shouted.

Ellie and I jumped but, before we could say anything, Mr Michael's stern face broke into a smile.

"I'm just kidding," he said, "Skungus loves to be stroked."

"Your dog is called Skungus?" Ellie asked.

"He sure is, Ferguson. Named after my dear old mother," Mr Michaels said. I couldn't tell if he was being serious or not and, by the confused look on her face, neither could Ellie.

"That was you that made that sound? The whistle?" Ellie asked.

Mr Michaels nodded, bending down to scratch Skungus between the ears.

"Gotta control him somehow," he said.

"Why do you have a dog in the school, sir?" I enquired.

"He works here," he replied matter-of-factly, as Skungus positioned himself between his legs.

"Works here? How can a dog have a job?" Ellie asked dismissively.

"He's not a teacher mind you, he's head of pest control and security. Plus, he's darn good company," Mr Michaels lifted the dog's face so their eyes met and he seemed to be talking directly to the animal. "Much better company than humans if you ask me." He broke the eye-contact with Skungus and stared straight at me and Ellie. The smile the dog had brought to Mr Michaels' face drained away as he spoke. "If I had it my way, I'd replace all you kids with dogs in a second. Nothing but dogs in the whole school. The whole town, preferably."

Ellie and I suddenly got the impression that our welcome had been outstayed so we beat a hasty retreat. Mr Michaels was only too eager to show us to the exit.

CHAPTER FIVE

AFTER LUNCH, I left Ellie and made my way to the changing rooms for my first ever P.E. lesson. I slipped into my school shorts and t-shirt as quickly as I could and followed the rest of the boys outside.

We formed two lines, one for boys and one for girls. I looked to my right and locked eyes with Zaza. She was the only friendly face in the gaggle of strangers. She nodded to the front and I looked just in time to see a stern-looking woman approaching. She wore an ill-fitting polo-shirt with the collar turned up and equally ill-fitting bright green shorts.

"EYES FRONT!" she bellowed. Everyone fell silent immediately and obeyed her orders. "Most of you know me," she continued at a lower volume. "But for the newcomers among you…" She looked directly at me. As far as I was aware, there weren't any other new students in this class. "My name is Mrs Harrison. I am your P.E. teacher. You will do exactly as I say, exactly when I say it. Do you understand?" There was a murmur of assent as kids looked at their shoes or off into the distance. "Great!" Mrs Harrison said, clapping her hands together. “Today, we are going to be using my favourite piece of apparatus, the Whirlybird!” For the first time, the students made a noise louder than a whisper as a groan filled the air. As I looked around, I could see the disappointment on their faces. “That’s the spirit!” Mrs Harrison said, turning on her heels. “Follow me!” The two lines of kids followed the teacher across the playground and towards what I thought was a climbing frame. As we approached, I could see several planks of wood suspended by ropes. “This, children, is the Whirlybird!” Mrs Harrison shouted as we came to a stop. “A work of my own invention, you’re going to love it, I can tell.” Someone behind me choked a laugh. “First of all, we need a volunteer to show everyone how it’s done. Mr Ferguson?” she said, looking straight at me again.

“Me?” I asked, looking around desperately.

“Yes, you’ve not done this before. Correct?” I shook my head. She knew I hadn’t. “This way then, come on,” she said, beckoning me forward. “This first exercise is called the swinging planks.”

“I can see why,” I muttered to myself, as several planks swung ominously back and forth in front of me.

“Go ahead and jump up onto this first one for me,” Mrs Harrison continued, her voice almost motherly. A sheep leading her lamb to slaughter. “All you have to do here is move from one plank to the next. Easy!” she said, patting me on the back.

I could feel the eyes of the whole class looking at me as I held on for dear life. My cheeks burned red as I glanced down at the next swinging plank. I reached out with my hand and grasped the rope it was attached to. Then, in one swift move, I swung my leg out and jumped towards it.

I fell flat on my face. The whole class erupted with laughter as I dusted myself off and looked up at Mrs Harrison.

"Not so easy, huh?" she said, yanking me to my feet. "The trick to this apparatus is to skip every other plank!"

"*Now* you tell me," I mumbled, looking where I'd fallen. The plank had simply given way beneath my feet. It was rigged to collapse under any pressure.

"Let's move on," Mrs Harrison said, almost sweetly. As if it wasn't her fault I had a mouth full of dirt. "This next puzzle is called The Doors of Truth!" she said, with a self-satisfied smile. She'd clearly spent a long time thinking up these names. Nine rickety wooden doors stood before me in rows of three. "All you have to do is get from one side to the other as quickly as possible."

I took a step forward and assessed the situation. It seemed simple enough. The doors were suspended about a metre in the air but all I had to do was keep my balance as I moved across the planks that connected them.

I moved to the first door and pulled the handle. It opened and swung easily free of the frame. This was easy.

"Quicker!" Mrs Harrison yelled.

I could hear a small giggle move among the onlooking students. I'd show them how quickly I can do this, I thought, before taking off in a sprint towards the next door. I pushed the handle down mid-stride, slammed straight into the door and flew backwards into the mud below. Laughter erupted again. The door was locked and didn't budge.

"The key to *this* one is knowing which doors to open," Mrs Harrison explained. "I designed the Whirlybird Climbing Frame to test students mentally as well as physically." I scrambled to my feet and looked around. Except for Zaza, the whole class was still laughing.

"Could you not have just told me that?" I said, forcing myself to stay calm.

"Ah, but then the lesson wouldn't have had such impact, so to speak," Mrs Harrison said. "Anyway, you're not seriously hurt. Come on, move aside to let the others have a go."

I brushed myself off and hastily joined the back of the queue, keeping my head down for the rest of the lesson. My knees were scuffed and my elbows were sore from where I'd landed. Mostly, however, I was annoyed that Mrs Harrison had set me up.

I vowed silently to myself that I never wanted to see the Whirlybird climbing frame again. I wanted to forget this lesson ever happened. Little did I know, the Whirlybird was to soon become more important than any of us could've realised.

The rest of the day went by without much excitement and soon we were heading home after our first day at our brand new school.

When we got back, I braced myself for our mum to greet us at the door with hugs, kisses and questions about our day. However, the questions never came and Mum simply gave us a quick smile before heading upstairs to sort through boxes.

"Well, that was easier than I thought," Ellie said, as we dumped her school things in her room. "I thought she'd be bugging us all afternoon."

"Yeah, I suppose she's still really busy from the move," I replied, nodding at the various cardboard boxes strewn about the hallway.

By dinner time, our dad had arrived home from his new job with the government and we braced ourselves for the inquisition we'd expected from Mum, but they were both strangely quiet as we sat down. I looked at the plate of creamy mash potatoes and meaty sausages in front of me and back up again. Mum and Dad smiled at me sweetly but still didn't speak.

"How was your new job, Dad?" I asked, feeling an awkwardness I'd never felt before with my parents. Normally, they were carefree and jovial. Most of the time, you couldn't stop my mum talking if you tried, and yet, today the atmosphere was different. It was frosty and unnatural. All smiles but no warmth.

"Fine, thank you," Dad replied, tersely. He was as polite as always but something wasn't right. He'd always taken an interest in my education before, but he didn't even ask how our first day at a new school was.

Something was very wrong.

CHAPTER SIX

THAT NIGHT, AFTER I closed my laptop and climbed into bed, my head swam with the events of the previous 12 hours. It had been a long day and I could feel myself drifting off to sleep as I glanced out the window of my new bedroom. The wind rustled the trees on the lawn outside and I noticed, for the first time, that I could see the school over the rooftops in the distance.

The unmistakable silhouette of the large school buildings stood proudly against the clear night sky. Almost all of the lights were off but, strangely, one or two were left on. I chuckled to myself as I thought of how mad Mr Michaels would be if he knew teachers were leaving lights on overnight.

Just as I was about to close my eyes to sleep, I saw something move in one of the illuminated classrooms. Surely, no teachers were working this late? I rubbed my eyes and looked again. There was definitely a figure moving through the school windows.

I looked down at the street below. Nothing stirred and everything was quiet. In the distance, a train rattled slowly by. I looked at the school again. The figure was still there, I was sure of it. Only, it was so far away that maybe I was mistaken? Maybe it was a curtain blowing in the wind, or a mannequin from a science lesson casting a shadow?

I strained my eyes to get a better look. It was moving. It was travelling from room to room, so it couldn't be a curtain or a mannequin. It was *alive*. Not only that, but it looked grotesque. It moved with an unnatural lilt. It hobbled and scraped its way clumsily around the school.

I forced myself to look away. I was being ridiculous. I was tired and my mind was playing tricks on me. I shut my eyes and forced myself to think about something else to get to sleep. A few seconds passed, or maybe it was hours, before suddenly I heard a blood-curdling scream ringing out from Ellie's room.

CHAPTER SEVEN

I THREW OFF my covers, jumped from my bed and ran as fast as I could to my sister's room. I burst through the door and saw Ellie sitting up in bed. She was breathing heavily and sweat was dripping from her forehead.

"What's wrong, Ellie? What is it?" I asked, urgently. She looked at me and then around the room. The house was still unfamiliar to us both.

"Are you okay?" I asked again. She finally seemed to register where she was.

"Yes, I think so. I just had a bad dream," she said, still visibly confused. "I was at the school and…"

"Darling, what is it!?" Mum had entered the room in a hurry. Dad followed sleepily after.

"Are you okay, sweetie?' he said, rubbing his eyes and stifling a yawn.

"Just a silly nightmare," Ellie replied, now with a slight smile. I knew Ellie would be okay so I turned to leave.

"Oh, my little princess, tell Mummy all about it." I reached the door handle and pulled.

"Well, I was at school and it was really dark."

I paused.

"And there was this thing. This *beast.*"

Chills ran across my skin.

"It was like a big dog. A werewolf!" Ellie continued.

I turned and re-entered the room. Dad suddenly seemed a lot more awake. Mum looked at him with wide, knowing eyes. There was something they weren't telling us.

"Don't worry about it, baby. You're right, it was just a silly dream," Dad said, trying his best to force a smile.

"That's right, back to bed now. You as well, Jack," Mum said, turning to me and ushering me out the door. I looked at Ellie and could tell she was thinking the same as me. Something wasn't right. As I stepped back over the threshold and into the hall, I glanced at my dad just in time to see his teeth had transformed into the long, thin fangs of a werewolf.

CHAPTER EIGHT

I LET OUT a low, inhuman scream and everyone in the room looked at me. I took a step back and looked at my dad again.

"What ish it, Jack?" he said with a lisp. I looked down at his mouth again and realised my mistake. He was wearing his retainer to bed. His doctor had prescribed it to help cure his tooth-ache.

I could feel myself turning red with embarrassment. As the moonlight reflected off the metal, my dad's retainer looked like fangs.

"I thought I saw a rat," I said, already turning back towards the hall and my own room.

There was a crispness in the air as Ellie and I set off for school together the next morning. We'd both slightly overslept so didn't have a chance to speak while devouring our cereal and rushing out the door. As we reached the end of our street and out of sight of the house, I looked at Ellie.

"I have to tell you something," I said in a hushed voice. Ellie studied my face. "It's about last night. I was looking out my window towards the school and I thought I saw something."

"You saw... *something?"* she asked, clearly confused by my agitated state.

"Yes, something unnatural. Something like what you saw in your dream." Ellie stopped walking and we stared at each other.

"My dream? The one about the werewolf?" she said, quizzically. "The school is miles away, how could you possibly see anything?"

"Well, it was more shadows and movement and..." Even as I spoke, I could tell how ridiculous it sounded now I said the words out loud.

"Are you sure you weren't dreaming, too?" Ellie said, kindly. "I mean, that Zaza girl had been talking about beasts hadn't she? She probably put the idea in our heads and we both dreamed about it. Dad always says you dream about what's on your mind."

She was right, of course she was. How could I have been so stupid? I was so tired from moving house and starting a new school that I must've been seeing things that weren't there. Maybe I was drifting in and out of sleep the whole time. It seemed so real but, then, dreams often do.

I dropped the subject and we continued walking to school. Thankfully, Ellie didn't bring it up again or make fun of me for it. I know if it was the other way around, I wouldn't have been able to resist cracking a few jokes at her expense.

We got to school and split off to our separate classes like before. As I entered the room, I was surprised to see that Zaza had moved to sit next to me.

"You came back then," she said, as I dropped into my seat and shoved my bag under the desk.

"Didn't really have a choice," I replied, smiling.

"Some kids don't come back, you know. They take one look at the place and run," Zaza said, her expressionless face not giving anything away.

"Can't imagine why," I replied, as Mr Cruft entered the class and everyone fell silent.

The teacher set his bag on his desk and scanned the room. He hesitated for a moment upon seeing Zaza's new location before continuing to set his things out with a wry smile on his face.

"Okay, everyone. Today we're going to start our reading of Dr Jekyll and Mr Hyde. But, first, I need a volunteer to help Mr Michaels here with a special project." Mr Cruft gestured to the classroom door where the janitor was stood with an unpleasant look on his face. "A volunteer, please." I looked around the class. Everyone had their head down in an attempt to avoid making eye contact with either of the adults. "Right, then I shall have to pick for you. Let's see… young Mr Ferguson," he said, as the slight smile returned to his ashen face. "It will be a good way for you to become more, uh, familiar with the grounds."

Zaza and I looked at each other. She seemed as unhappy about the situation as I did.

"Right then, come along," Mr Michaels grunted.

I collected my things and left the class as the rest of the students looked on in silence. We left the school buildings and started walking across the playing fields towards a high fence on the other side.

"Excuse me, sir," I asked weakly, as Mr Michaels marched several paces in front.

"Yes, what is it?" He answered without breaking stride.

"May I ask where we're going? What we're doing?" I said as we trudged across the muddy football pitch. The janitor stopped and waited for me to catch up before gesturing towards a fence in the distance. I squinted and strained to get a closer look.

"That," he said, brushing a tangle of grey hair from his eyes, "is what we're doing. We're fixing the darn fences. I need an idiot like you to hold them in place while I drive in the nails."

As we finally got close enough I could see the extent of the damage. The fence panels were bent and broken in all different directions and lumps of turf had been ripped from the ground. Mud tracks led in a multitude of directions and broken branches littered the earth.

"What happened here?" I said, curiously.

"Darn kids, I expect. Happened overnight," replied Mr Michaels, hesitating slightly before he spoke. "But that's not important right now. What's important is you do as I say. Grab those planks." He pointed to a pile of wood neatly stacked near the broken fence. "And hold them in place while I get the hammer."

I slung my bag off my shoulder and got to work. The morning sun was breaking through the tree-line and its warmth was a welcome change from the stuffy classroom. Once Mr Michaels had repaired one bit of the fence, we moved swiftly on to the next. We soon developed a smooth rhythm and the fences came together quickly. After twenty or so minutes, I stepped back and wiped the sweat from my brow.

"Mr Michaels?" I said, tentatively.

"Yes?" he replied, with a nail hanging from his lips and a hammer in his hand.

"It's hot. Is there anything to drink?"

Mr Michaels stopped what he was doing and looked back and forth between me and the fence. I was exhausted from lifting and holding all the wood.

"Oh right, yes. I mean, no. Not here. Go get some water from the canteen and bring it back here for both of us. No, wait! I'm the adult. I'll go." He puffed his chest out and strode back across the field towards the school without so much as a backward glance.

"What a weird guy," I thought as I watched him leave.

I sat under a large willow tree that reminded me of one outside our old house. It was still early but the heat from the sun had sapped my energy.

I looked around me at the damaged fence and trees. Was it really possible that kids could have caused all this mess? As I was thinking, I suddenly became aware of a rustling sound coming from a nearby bush.

"It's probably the wind. Or a dog," I said aloud to myself, trying desperately to ignore my unease.

Suddenly, the noise grew louder as something burst out from the shadows. I screamed and jumped to the side. I span round to face the noise and all my breath left me as I looked up to see the gigantic figure of a werewolf pouncing out from behind the bush.

CHAPTER NINE

I STUMBLED BACKWARDS and tripped over a fallen branch. The dark figure was bearing down on me. I tried to scream but no sound came out. I scrambled for something to defend myself with but as I looked back, I realised the creature wasn't growling - it was laughing. Its sharp teeth weren't sharp. Its red eyes weren't red. It wasn't a werewolf, it was Mr Michaels.

The janitor stood over me laughing maniacally.

"Got ya!" he screamed joyously. "You should've seen your face!"

"Very funny," I said, brushing myself down.

"Here's your water," Mr Michael's said when he eventually stopped laughing. "Try not to scream when I pass it to you."

I felt the blood rushing to my face again.

"Yeah, well, I was only scared because of your ugly face!" I said angrily. Mr Michaels stopped chuckling to himself and looked me dead in the eyes.

"Well, well, the boy has grown a backbone," he snarled. "But you know what backbones get you? Detention. Tomorrow night, after school."

I was tempted to double-down and insult him again but something about the look in his eyes told me it wasn't a good idea so I bit my tongue. I could feel the anger still boiling inside of me but I managed to keep it in check as we got back to work.

We continued building the fence in silence. It became harder and more uncomfortable as the morning passed and the sun rose higher in the sky. Eventually, the fence was fixed and we progressed to clearing the fallen branches and raking the muddy tracks.

Before long, the patch of earth looked as good as new and Mr Michaels told me to gather my things and follow him back to class. In the rush to keep up with the janitor's long strides, I realised I'd left my bag behind when we were halfway across the field. I told Mr Michaels what happened before running back by myself to get my backpack.

As I reached the fence, the air around me suddenly seemed a lot chillier. A storm was coming. The bushes swayed violently and the wind whistled through the thicket. I saw my bag laying under the willow tree and bent down to pick it up. As I did, I heard another noise. An unnatural one. I stepped back. I could hear a rumbling sound coming from within the undergrowth.

"Very funny, Mr Michaels. You're not going to get me again!" I shouted, but as I turned to leave I saw Mr Michaels still waiting for me in the distance. I turned to the bush again and saw something standing right in front of me. Two bright red eyes stared out of the greenery. Its lips pulled back and I saw its razor-sharp teeth. It took a slow, deliberate step forward.

CHAPTER TEN

I REALISED MY only hope was to run. I turned on my heels and sprinted as fast as I could back across the playing field. I tripped. I hit the ground hard and instinctively rolled over to protect myself from the beast but it wasn't there. I looked back at the bushes. It had vanished. The leaves swayed gently in the cool breeze.

I wasn't going to wait for it to come back so I hauled myself up and carried on running to Mr Michaels. As I arrived, I could see on his face that he'd been laughing at me from a distance but I didn't care. I had to tell him.

"A werewolf! A real werewolf! In the bushes!" I pointed back the way I'd come as I struggled to catch my breath.

"A …werewolf?" Mr Michaels asked, his smile suddenly fading. "Are you sure?"

"Yes, I'm sure. It stood right in front of me."

The janitor took a deep breath and composed himself.

"Werewolves don't exist. And if they did, they wouldn't be out in the daytime scaring kids with their big teeth and bright red eyes."

"But sir," I said, "how did you know it had red eyes?"

CHAPTER ELEVEN

MR MICHAELS PEERED at me with a strange, fearful look on his face.

"Sir, how did you know it had big red eyes?" I repeated.

"I, uh, didn't," he stammered. "They always have red eyes, don't they? In the films, I mean. It doesn't matter, I need to go. I need to do some real work, not this babysitting stuff! Take the tools back to the shed and get back to your class. Now!"

The janitor dropped his tool bag at my feet and made a hasty retreat after pointing me in the direction of a rickety-looking shed in the shadow of one of the school's main buildings. As I approached the wooden shack, the courtyard was deserted. I could see the kids preparing to leave their classes through the greasy window panes and realised it was almost break time. I'd spent the whole lesson helping Mr Michaels.

I hurried towards the tool shed so I could be out in time to enjoy the break with Ellie. A padlock hung loose on the latch. I grabbed the door and pulled. It creaked loudly as I forced open its rusted hinges and stepped inside.

The interior was dark and smelled of sour milk and wet paint. I took a step forward and allowed my eyes to adjust to the light. The shed was crowded with random objects stacked from floor to ceiling. As I stepped further inside, the floorboards groaned under my weight and a pile of boxes swayed dangerously to my left. I looked around for a place to lay Mr Michaels' tool bag. Eventually, I saw a lone gap in the mess towards the back and pressed on.

I reached the rear of the shed, brushed the cobwebs from my face, and placed Mr Michaels' tools on the shelf. In an instant, it went dark. The light from the opening had disappeared. I peered into the blackness and figured the door must have blown shut in the wind.

With only a few thin beams of light breaking through cracks to guide me, I stepped towards the exit. I moved, arms stretched, feeling my way back. With the door shut, the outside world seemed further away. The school seemed to float far into the distance and the only existence was the here and now. The sound of my footsteps echoed around the room and every groan and crackle of the wood reverberated through my entire body. It wasn't until I was halfway towards the exit that I saw it.

One of the beams of sunlight was extinguished for a split second. Someone was outside the shed. I shouted, asking who was there. Hoping they'd open the door and allow me to see where I was going, but no-one answered.

I called out again.

Silence.

Another beam of light flickered. They were circling the shed, on the outside looking in.

"Sir? Is that you?" I called. "Ellie? Zaza?"

My voice wavered. I heard a reply, but it wasn't human.

CHAPTER TWELVE

THE BEAST PAWED and sniffed at the outside of the shed. Its claws scratched and splintered the wood. I felt my heart racing in my chest as I froze on the spot and listened intently. The werewolf was circling, biding its time. It was playing with its food.

I thought about the kids I'd seen through the windows. Surely, they would be leaving their classes any minute now and would scare the beast away? I couldn't wait to find out. The creature could burst through the flimsy wooden walls any second. I had to get out.

I took a step in the direction of the door, taking care to not make a sound. The floor sighed beneath my feet and I paused before trying again. A step further and I saw the slightest slither of light creeping under the doorway. I'd found the way out.

I felt the shelves around me and grabbed something cylindrical. A paint can, probably. I set myself in an amateur sprinter's pose and prepared mentally.

Suddenly, with the beast somewhere outside, I threw the can as hard as I could over my shoulder and ran forward towards the door. I heard the can crash into the back wall and cause an avalanche of school supplies. Hoping it was enough to distract the beast, I lunged for the exit. I burst through the door and was blinded by sunlight as I ran desperately towards the school buildings.

CHAPTER THIRTEEN

NOT KNOWING IF I was safe or not, I kept running, turned the corner and - *BANG* - crashed right into Ellie.

"Jack! It's me. Calm down," Ellie said, gripping me by the shoulders. "What's wrong?"

I paused to catch my breath as I surveyed the scene around me. Students and teachers were flooding out of the classrooms and filling every bit of available space. I rushed to the corner of the building and looked back towards the shed. There was no sign of the beast. It must have fled when it saw so many people.

"Jack!" Ellie shouted, bringing me out of my frenzied state.

"Sorry, Ellie," I said, forcing myself to stop and take a breath. "I've had a hell of a morning."

Ellie looked at me and smiled. I took her by the arm and led her towards the middle of the courtyard so that we were completely surrounded by people.

"I need to tell you something, Ellie. It's going to sound crazy but just hear me out."

Ellie nodded and smiled again. You could always rely on my sister to be kind and understanding. I told her what had happened in the playing fields. I told her about the beast in the bush and about how strangely Mr Michaels reacted. I told her about the shed and how I had to run away from the werewolf. I stopped talking and studied her face. She stared silently back at me, taking it all in.

"I need to sit down," she said, finding a gap on the nearby wall. Ellie was a year younger than me but she was much smarter. If anyone knew what to do, she would. "In the field," she added, still trying to make sense of it all. "The beast. It came from the bush?" I nodded. "And you got a clear look at its body?"

"Well, I saw its face. Then I ran," I said, trying to think back.

"And in the shed, what did you see? I mean, really *see,*" she asked.

"I saw… its shadow. And I heard it! It snorted and it scratched and the walls."

Ellie nodded, deep in concentration.

"You know what, I saw something, too," she said softly. "I saw Zaza walking across the courtyard halfway through the morning lesson."

Ellie looked up and it suddenly dawned on me. She had solved the problem of the school werewolf.

CHAPTER FOURTEEN

"IT'S ZAZA!" WE said, simultaneously.

It was so obvious. Zaza had been pranking us from the start. There was a reason the other kids didn't want to sit next to her. She had been planning this all along. First, she planted the idea in our heads when she started talking about beasts in the school. Then, she dressed up as a werewolf and jumped out from the bushes to scare me before finally shutting me in the shed and making growling noises on the outside.

"I've got to admit, she got me good!" I said, puffing out my cheeks. "She truly had me believing in werewolves for a second there."

"How do you think she got excused from class?" Ellie said, the facts still whirring around her head.

"I have no idea, but I think we should find out."

Over Ellie's shoulder, I saw Zaza making her way across the courtyard. We ran to catch her up.

"You think you're funny, huh?" I said, stopping her in her tracks.

"I'm sorry, what?"

"We know it's you," Ellie added.

"What is me?" Zaza asked.

"Scaring us!" I said, half shouting.

"*Trying* to scare us," Ellie corrected.

"Right, right. *Trying,"* I said, almost convincingly.

"Guys, I don't know what you're on about. Has something happened?" Zaza said, acting innocent. She could've won an Oscar, she was acting so well.

"In the playing fields and by the shed. You're not fooling us," I said proudly.

"We saw you leaving class!" Ellie added, triumphantly. We had her now. There was no way she could deny it.

"Jack. Ellie. I left class because I was feeling sick. The nurse gave me some headache tablets. Look." She thrust her hand in her pocket and produced a pack of four pills, two of which were missing. "Anyway, I don't have time for this. I'm going home early, my mum's waiting for me. I'll see you both tomorrow."

Zaza left and carried on walking towards the car park. I looked at Ellie.

"We did the right thing, didn't we?" I asked eventually.

"Definitely! You're not buying that nonsense about the headache tablets, are you? She just made it all up!"

I didn't know what to think. Before we spoke to her, I was sure it was Zaza pranking us but her denial seemed so genuine. After she left, Ellie and I barely spoke for the rest of the day.

The afternoon passed quickly and soon we were arriving back home. I kicked off my shoes, went straight up to my room and crashed out on the bed. Looking up at the ceiling, I could see pale yellow stains left by the previous occupants. The house needed redecorating and we hadn't even started on the upstairs yet. Suddenly, I got the urge to escape my dull, grey bedroom and relax outside. The garden was the only part of the property that the previous owners seemed to care about. The lawn was immaculately shaped and trimmed and the flowers around the edge were bright and vivacious.

I left my room still wearing my school uniform, grabbed my tablet and headed downstairs towards the back door. After a long day, there would be nothing I'd like more than to hang out in the hammock while I listen to music and talk to my friends back home.

I walked through the kitchen and Mum did a double-take as she saw where I was heading.

"Where are you going?" she asked, mild panic in her voice.

"…outside?" I replied, not quite sure why she would care.

"Wait," she said, placing her hand on the door. "Help me with the cooking first? Please."

There was a strange look in her eyes. She was worried. I stopped and looked out towards the garden. The daffodils swayed gently in the breeze as the setting sun fought its way through the trees. Our friendly neighbour, Mr Ramsey, pottered on his side of the fence. What could my mum possibly be concerned about? I didn't know, but I could tell she was serious. I put my tablet down and helped her peel potatoes.

I spent the rest of the evening in my room watching videos and listening to music. The events of the day bounced around inside my head as I thought about everything from the morning fixing fences to the look on my mum's face when I went to go out into the garden. I wished I could go back to our old house where things made sense.

Eventually, the sun set and the sound from passing cars stopped completely. I looked at the clock and yawned. I wriggled out of my clothes and slipped under the covers. My bed was the one piece of furniture in the room that had come from our old house and it was my favourite place in the entire universe. It was my own little oasis in a strange and confusing world. I rolled over, stretched my arms and legs out fully and shut my eyes.

My peace didn't last long. In the hallway, I could hear a peculiar noise. Someone was hanging around outside my door.

"Go away!" I yelled.

No answer. I could hear them moving, bumping into things. I realised I was going to have to deal it directly so I threw off my covers and got to my feet. I grabbed the handle and swung the door open.

"WOULD YOU PLEASE STOP MAKING SO MUCH…"

I looked around but there was no-one there. The hallway was completely empty. I peered over the bannister and could see flickering blue and yellow light coming from the TV. Mum and Dad liked to stay up late and binge-watch their favourite shows. I thought the noise was right outside my room, but I must've been hearing the TV.

I shut the door and went back to bed, but as soon as my head hit the pillow, the noise started again. I realised it must be Ellie playing a prank on me. I got up to confront her and swung the door open again. Only, this time, the hallway wasn't empty. Standing in front of me was my dad. I looked up at him. He stared back at me. Something wasn't right.

"Dad, are you okay? You scared me."

He didn't answer. He just stared. Then, slowly, he lifted his leg and took a step towards me. I looked at his face. This wasn't my dad. This was someone, or *something*, else. He opened his mouth and I gasped. His teeth were long and pointy. He took another step towards me and the light from the moon shone on his bright, red eyes.

CHAPTER FIFTEEN

I STEPPED BACK as he crossed the threshold into my room.

"Dad? What's wrong? What's happening?" I asked, but he didn't answer. Instead, he stumbled forward and lunged towards me. I leapt to the side and his arms swung wildly past my face. "Dad, stop it!" I yelled as the fear rose inside me.

He turned to face me again. His red eyes were staring intently but I got the impression he wasn't fully conscious. He didn't know what he was doing. My dad would never hurt me intentionally.

"It's me, Dad! It's Jack!" I screamed, but it didn't make any difference. He lunged again. This time, the tips of his fingers scratched my cheek as I barely managed to evade his grasp. I felt my face. It was hot with blood. His hands were no longer human, they were claws with huge, yellow nails curling around the ends.

I stumbled and fell. On my back, I looked up to see it advancing on me again. I searched the room for any means of escape. The window was blocked, but there was a chance I could make it to the door. The beast flung itself towards me with a growl. I rolled to the side and heard it crash into my TV, but I didn't look back. I was up and running for the door.

I surged out onto the landing and raced down the stairs. I had to get help. I had to tell Mum. I reached the bottom floor and turned the corner into the living room. The TV was still on, but Mum wasn't watching it. I whirled around on the spot. My dad was thumping his way down the stairs, but he wasn't alone.

Mum was next to him. Her face was almost unrecognisable, but it was definitely her. Her teeth were pointed, her back was hunched. She turned to look at my dad and then, together, they howled at the moon.

CHAPTER SIXTEEN

"JACK!" ELLIE SAID. "Wake up. We're gonna be late for school."

I opened my eyes and looked around the room. I was in bed. The TV was still intact. Nothing had changed from the night before.

"Where's Mum and Dad?" I asked, my head still fuzzy.

"Mum's downstairs making breakfast and Dad's gone to work as usual. Get up, we're gonna be late!" Ellie said again.

It was all a dream. A nightmare. Other than being sweaty and late, I was fine. Ellie made her way downstairs as I got up and changed. She wasn't lying, we really were running late. I rushed around brushing my teeth and washing my face before joining the others downstairs with minutes to spare. Mum was in the kitchen with a plateful of scrambled eggs laid out for me.

"Hello, sweetie," she said, gripping me tight in a hug. "Eggs here for you. Your favourite."

"Thanks, Mum," I replied, "But I don't really have time."

"Nonsense!" she said, practically forcing me into the seat and placing a fork in my hands.

"Breakfast is the most important meal of the day. And anyway, I wanted to make you something nice. I know this move hasn't been easy on either of you."

I looked across the table at Ellie scoffing down the last of her plate. I looked back at Mum. She was smiling, but still looked sad.

"Mum, we're fine. Are you? You seem a little …off," I asked, placing one of my hands on hers.

Mum was clearly surprised by the question. She took a second, glancing down into her lap.

"I'm fine, baby. It's just been very stressful moving house. And your father has been stressed at his new job. There are a lot of problems he has to sort out there. But, we'll be fine. I promise," she squeezed my hand and smiled. "You're not to go worrying about us. Do you understand? We're fine. Just enjoy yourself at school and look after your sister for me, okay?"

"Jack!" Ellie said, suddenly. "The time!"

I looked at my watch. We were really late now.

"I'm sorry, Mum. I haven't got time for the eggs. See you later!" I yelled, as we hurried out the door.

As I left the house, Ellie was waiting out front straddling her bicycle and holding mine up next to her.

"We'll get there quicker like this," she said, "We'll chain them up outside the front gates."

I jumped on my bike and set off for school. We always used to ride to our old school in the morning, but we hadn't seen anyone else doing it here. As usual, the journey quickly turned into a race between us. I powered past Ellie as we left our road. I had the explosive speed, but Ellie knew she had the endurance. She bided her time waiting for me to tire myself out, but I was determined it wasn't going to work this time.

I kept up the pace as we rounded another corner. Ellie was a few meters back but she was sticking with me. My thighs began to burn. If I slowed down now, Ellie would cruise past. I put my head down, gritted my teeth and carried on peddling at full speed. I glanced at my watch. We were making record time but were still on course to be late.

"This way!" I shouted to Ellie, as I took a shortcut across a field. She followed and we darted through some overgrown moorland, avoiding shrubs and low hanging trees. The crisp morning air was biting at my cheeks and I could feel my lips starting to dry out.

Eventually, the undergrowth cleared and the route ahead came into view. The school rose up over the horizon as I looked at my watch again. We were going to make it on time if we could just keep up the pace for the final push.

I looked back over my shoulder. Ellie was gaining on me. The energy she had saved earlier on was paying off and the distance between us was closing. My chest stung as I sucked in air to catch my breath. I was determined to reach the school before my sister.

I stood up on the peddles and pushed hard through the pain barrier. We careened across the ground, getting closer and closer to the school. One last effort and we'd be there. I swerved left to avoid a bush, then right to clear a ditch and then… something happened.

In a split second, I was no longer riding my bike but flying through the air. Something had jumped out in front of us. I hit the ground hard and kept rolling. Dust and dirt flew up in a cloud around me as I came screeching to halt.

A few seconds passed before the pain hit me. My knees and elbows stung intensely. My head was heavy and my sight was blurred. I looked around me and saw Ellie in a pile close by. She'd fallen too. I was about to call out to her when I saw something out the corner of my eye. I turned my head to see the dark, gangly figure of a werewolf slinking off into the distance.

CHAPTER SEVENTEEN

I TURNED BACK to Ellie and called her name. I scrambled to my feet and edged closer to my sister as she lay on the floor. Her bike was upturned and wedged in a bush. The dust around us was still settling.

"Ellie. Are you okay?"

She rolled over and looked up at me.

"What… was that?" she asked, still dazed from the crash.

"I don't know," I said, honestly. "Something ran out in front of us."

"It looked like a…" I knew what she was going to say before she said it. "Werewolf!"

"I saw something," I confessed. "Just now, moving that way. It looked like one of them."

"But, it can't be. Can it? It was Zaza pranking us, wasn't it?" Ellie said, sitting up and tugging her dirty blonde hair back into place.

"That's what I thought, but then…" I stopped and listened. Something made a noise nearby.

"What was that?" Ellie whispered.

I looked around. My head was still throbbing. There was no one around us.

"Let's go. Quickly." I said, giving Ellie a hand up.

"We're really late now," she said, hurrying to jerk her bike out the bush.

I picked up my own bike and noticed the chain had snapped in two. There was no way I was riding it until that was fixed. We were just starting to push our bikes towards school when we heard it again. Something was in the bushes. It had been watching us the whole time.

CHAPTER EIGHTEEN

I HEARD A growl. I spun around and saw its ears poking out the bush. I stumbled backwards and fell over my bike. Ellie screamed. We braced ourselves as the beast emerged. We soon realised our mistake.

Skungus, the janitor's dog, came bounding out of the bush wagging his tail. Ellie and I looked at each other and breathed a sigh of relief. Skungus was on us now, licking our faces.

"Nasty fall, that."

We turned to see Mr Michaels standing behind us.

"Saw it all, I did," he said, leaning on a stick.

We grunted and got to our feet. Skungus skipped happily back to his master.

"You saw the whole thing?" Ellie said. "All of it?"

I suddenly realised what she was getting at. If Mr Michaels saw the crash, he must've seen if a werewolf jumped out in front of us.

"Like I said. I saw it," he replied, softly. "From a distance of course. Up at the school, we were."

"So, you saw what jumped out on us? What caused the crash?" I asked, trying my best not to influence his answer.

"And what was it!?" Ellie added, practically shouting.

Mr Michaels paused.

"Hard to say," he said, finally. "Could've been an animal."

I looked at my sister.

"Could've been someone wanting you to think they were an animal," Mr Michaels added.

"Which was it?" I asked, frantically.

"I don't know," he said, with a sigh. "What I do know is, if it *was* an animal, then it's my job to worry about it, isn't it? If it was a kid, then you're on your own. I couldn't care less."

I heard someone panting heavily and realised it was me. I was still out of breath. I took a second to regain my composure as no-one spoke.

"Another thing I do know," Mr Michaels added, with a sinister smile. "Is that school started four minutes ago. That's a detention for you both."

Ellie and I exchanged a disbelieving glance. Was he really going to punish us after he saw the crash?

"You're already penned in for a detention this afternoon, Mr Ferguson. You can join him, young Elsa."

"Ellie. My name's Ellie," she said, sharply.

"Right. Ellie," Mr Michaels said. "You can join your brother in detention, *Ellie*."

Mr Michaels tramped away and Skungus followed, his tail wagging happily in the morning air.

"Can you believe that guy?" I scoffed, picking up my bike again.

"He's right, though," Ellie said, deep in thought.

"He's *right!?* You want to have detention?"

"No, not about that. Obviously, he's an idiot for giving us detention. I mean he's right about the …thing that jumped out at us." I didn't follow. "What I mean is," she added, sensing my confusion. "if it was a person trying to scare us again, it's up to us to deal with it, isn't it?"

She was right. This had gone on long enough and it was getting dangerous.

"We could've been seriously injured in that crash," Ellie said, somehow knowing what I was thinking.

"It's Zaza, isn't it?" I said, the realisation slowly dawning on me.

CHAPTER NINETEEN

WE FINALLY ARRIVED at school and chained our bikes up outside. The courtyard was empty and ominously quiet. The thought of entering the class while it was already underway filled me with dread. I arranged to meet up with Ellie again at break time and we went our separate ways. I knocked twice on the door and pushed it open with the back of my hand.

"Ah, Mr Ferguson. So good of you to join us," Mr Cruft sneered. "And how lovely of you to dress up for the occasion," he said, looking down at my scuffed clothing and messy hair. I heard a muffled snigger from the back of the room.

I took my seat next to Zaza. I noticed as I sat down that her shoes were caked with mud. I looked up and saw her staring back at me. We locked eyes for a second before Mr Cruft started talking. Eventually, we were assigned work to do and the class erupted into chatter. I looked straight at Zaza.

"I know it was you," I said, my teeth clenched.

Zaza looked at me and sighed.

"What now?" she replied, with a tone of irritation in her voice.

"Jumping out at us before school. It's not funny, we could've been really hurt," I said, quickly.

"I don't know what you're talking about, Jack! Why are you accusing me of these weird things again?"

"So, you're telling me your shoes are like that because you went for a morning run across a muddy bog? A casual bit of exercise in your school clothes?"

Zaza looked down at her feet and tried to kick some of the mud off.

"That is none of your business," she said as her cheeks flushed red. "I've had these shoes a long time, they get muddy sometimes."

I wasn't buying it. She was lying to my face.

"It's not funny," I said again. "Ellie fell really hard. We both did."

"Ellie? Is she okay?" Zaza said, suddenly taking more of an interest in the conversation. The thought of her pretending to care about Ellie made me angrier than I had been before. Suddenly, I felt heat rising to my face. Zaza had put me in danger, put my little sister in danger, and now she was sat next to me pretending to be concerned.

"Just because you don't have any friends," I spat. "You think it's okay to pick on other people? Well, it's not!"

Zaza looked at me with wide, doleful eyes. She was a great actor. For a split second, I really believed she was hurt by my words and I started to feel bad. However, then something changed in her face. She stood up straight and pushed my books off the desk.

The other students stopped and stared. The room was weirdly quiet.

"I'm glad you fell. I'm glad it hurt," she said, tears welling in her eyes. "I'll do it again and, next time, you won't be so lucky."

CHAPTER TWENTY

"THAT'S ENOUGH FROM you!" Mr Cruft's voice boomed out. "Detention. After school today."

Zaza looked stared at him intently. Her eyes were narrow and her brow was furrowed. She was still standing at her desk as the whole class looked on. Her hair was wild and she clenched her fists. After a second that felt like an eternity, she seemed to realise where she was, snatched up her books and stomped off to sit at the back of the class again.

I knew I had probably gone too far but I was too mad to care. The thought of Zaza hurting Ellie made me lose any sympathy I might have felt for her. I sat silently at my desk for the rest of the lesson and stormed out of class as the bell rang for break.

I met Ellie as planned and told her all about what happened with Zaza. I'd calmed down since the argument and doubts had started to creep into my head.

"Don't feel bad, Jack," Ellie said. "She started all this. We didn't do anything to her and she's gone out her way to scare us."

"You weren't there, though. She looked like she was going to cry."

"Look at your arms," Ellie said, gesturing to my cuts and grazes. "She did that!"

"I know. It's just that, I don't think she's a bad person. Maybe it was just a prank gone wrong?"

Ellie considered what I'd said. She had been angrier than I'd seen her in a long time, but she was never mean. I knew she'd see the good in people if it was there.

"You're right," she said, finally. "She was probably just trying to make friends in her own… special way?"

I laughed.

"We should talk to her again," I said.

"Try to make things right between us," Ellie added, with a smile.

We knew Zaza liked to hang out by herself on the other side of the main building so we set off across the courtyard. As we turned the corner, the number of students milling about dropped off until there was only a handful left. The roar of other kids died away and people looked at us as if we were intruding on something secret.

Zaza wasn't anywhere to be seen but we kept going. Eventually, I heard someone call my name from behind us and span around. As I did, a shadowy figure leapt out from behind a wall and screamed. I jumped back and tripped over a rock. Ellie scrambled backwards too. The beast advanced on us with its fangs bare. Then it laughed.

Zaza pulled the mask off and looked down at me. All the kids in the area realised what had happened and burst into hysterical laughter. I could feel the blood rising to my cheeks.

"Watch out, Ferguson! The beast'll get ya!" Zaza shouted. The kids laughed again. I jumped to my feet and took a step towards Zaza, but Ellie jumped between us.

"It's not worth it, Jack. Let's go," she said, looking back at Zaza. She led me away from the scene as I brushed myself down and tried to calm my nerves.

"How could you just walk away like that?" I said to Ellie as we arrived back at the central courtyard.

"We need to be smart about this," she replied, with a twinkle in her eyes. "We'll get her back. We just need to bide our time."

She looked at me and smiled.

"I've got an idea."

CHAPTER TWENTY-ONE

"WE NEED TO give Zaza a taste of her own medicine," Ellie said.

"And how are we going to do that?" I asked.

"We've all got detention together after school, right?"

"Right."

"And you've got art class this afternoon, correct?"

"Correct."

"Pick these things up from the communal supply cupboard." Ellie grabbed a scrap of paper from her bag and began scribbling. "Meet me by Mr Michaels' shed at the final bell. We'll have ten minutes to sort it all out before detention starts!"

She looked at me and giggled.

"This is going to be great!" she said, tugging at my sleeve before running off to her next lesson.

The afternoon passed by slowly but, eventually, the bell rang and I met back up with Ellie. My backpack was full of random items. I emptied it out onto the floor. Superglue, facepaint, felt. What on earth was she planning?

"Fantastic!" she said happily. "This is perfect!"

She grabbed the items and started hastily affixing them to various parts of her body.

"What are you doing?" I asked.

"You'll see!" She answered as she stuck some fur to her forehead.

Two minutes later and Ellie was transformed. She was no longer my scruffy little sister. She now looked like a tiny werewolf.

"Ta-da!" she said, spinning on the spot. "And for the final touch, I got these from the drama club." She reached into her bag and produced a set of very real-looking fangs.

"Amazing!" I said, taking it all in. "You're a bit smaller than the real thing, but I know just what to do. You climb up on that ledge over there, I'll bring Zaza round the corner and you can jump down at us. That way, she won't even notice you're a little girl."

Werewolf Ellie giggled.

"Thith will teach her to scare us!" she said, the plastic fangs filling her mouth.

Ellie clambered into position and I waited around the corner. A few seconds later, Zaza appeared.

"What's so funny?" she said, seeing the smile on my face.

"Nothing," I said, plainly.

I wouldn't have been smiling if I knew what was about to happen.

CHAPTER TWENTY-TWO

ZAZA AND I walked side-by-side towards the corner behind which Ellie waited. In a few moments, we would have our revenge. For all the times that Zaza scared us, every scratch and bruise we got from the bike crash, the humiliation of being laughed at. It was all about to be avenged. As soon as we turned the corner, Zaza would be so frightened by Ellie's werewolf costume that we'd be even. Once we'd stopped laughing, that is.

We walked in silence. I still wasn't talking to Zaza after her latest stunt. As we approached the corner I fought with myself to hold in the laughter. I mustn't give the game away now.

I kept my cool and we moved closer and closer to the corner of the building. Two more meters and we'd be there. It was so close.

"Where do you think you're going!?" Mr Michaels' voice made us jump.

We turned around to see him standing a short distance away with a mop and bucket under his arms.

"No cushy detention for you today! This way. You've got some cleaning to do."

I panicked. Mr Michaels had arrived five minutes early. Ellie was still dressed as a werewolf. If the janitor saw her now, we'd be in even more trouble. I had to warn her. She had so much fake fur in her ears, there's no way she'd have heard what was happening.

"Sir, I forgot my bag. I'll just go get it," I said, hoping it'd be the perfect excuse to go and tell Ellie.

"I don't think so, Ferguson. Your belongings will still be there when we're done. Get moving. This way."

Mr Michaels led us halfway across the school.

"Wasn't there supposed to be three of you?" he said, as we reached the far end of the playground.

Zaza and I looked at each other, then back at Mr Michaels.

"I'm not sure, sir," Zaza said.

After everything that had happened, she was covering for Ellie. I could've kissed her.

"I don't know either, sir," I added.

Suddenly, I started to feel bad about our plan to scare Zaza. If I could get a message to Ellie, I'd tell her to call the whole thing off.

"Hmm, I'm sure there were three names on the list. I'll go check. You two, start scrubbing this floor."

"You want us to wash the playground?" Zaza asked.

"That's right. Get to it. I'll be right back."

Mr Michaels left. The playground became a lot quieter with only me and Zaza in it. We hesitated, looking at the mop and bucket. I wanted to thank her for not getting Ellie in more trouble, but I was still angry at her for scaring me earlier in the day. Plus, my mind was still preoccupied thinking about Ellie. She was, presumably, still dressed as a werewolf and waiting for Zaza to come around the corner. The thought of her cramped on that ledge with big furry ears and fake teeth made me laugh, but I knew she would get into deep trouble if she was caught.

I decided I had to tell Zaza. She might be able to help. Maybe we could work together, one of us distracting Mr Michaels while the other goes to find Ellie. The atmosphere was still tense, neither of us had spoken since the detention started. I reached for the bucket. Zaza reached for it at the same time.

"Zaza, I need to tell you something," I mumbled, breaking the silence.

"About the bucket? Just take it, man," she said.

"No, not about the bucket! About Ellie…" I struggled to arrange the words in my head.

"She's waiting for, she's on a ledge, fur and glue and…"

"What the hell are you talking about?" Zaza said, quite understandably. I wasn't making any sense.

"It's Ellie, she's… wait. What was that?"

Zaza heard it too. There was a low rumbling coming from a bush at the edge of the playground. I'd heard this before, I knew what it was. But, surely it couldn't be? It was Zaza playing a prank on us before but she was right next to me.

"Wow," I thought. Ellie is really committed to scaring Zaza. When she sets her mind to something, there's no stopping her. She must've heard Mr Michaels telling us to come here and then sneaked around him without being seen. All so she could jump out and get our revenge on Zaza.

I laughed to myself as Zaza looked around for the source of the noise. The wind had picked up and there was a chill in the air. Mr Michaels was long gone and we were the only people around.

The bush shook. Ellie was making this feel real. The growl reverberated around the playground. Zaza looked at me with wide eyes.

"Maybe we should head back to find Mr Michaels," she said. "He's been gone a long time and…"

"I think we should wait right here," I replied, remembering the laughter when Zaza scared me earlier.

The sound from the bush grew louder. Ellie was really laying it on thick. The bush rattled again. A big, black paw thudded down. I couldn't remember Ellie making paws from the art supplies. Another leg came out the bush. Thick and hairy. I couldn't remember Ellie using that much padding.

Then I saw its bright, red eyes and realised it wasn't Ellie.

CHAPTER TWENTY-THREE

THE BEAST STOOD upright. Its grotesque body stretched out until it towered above both of us. Drool hung low from its mouth. There was no mistaking this one, I could see right past its fangs and down its gaping throat. This was very big and very real.

I screamed. Zaza screamed. We turned and ran. I sprinted towards the school buildings. I could hear the beast behind us. It roared.

"Split up!" I shouted, over the chaos.

Zaza must've heard me because she bent her run and headed towards the left-hand side of the school as I continued to the right. The werewolf followed me.

I ran at full speed towards the school. My lungs began to sting as I searched for breath. My knees shuddered and my feet slapped heavily on the pavement. Finally, I slammed into a set of big double doors and frantically yanked them open. The werewolf was right behind me, I smelled its stale musk as I ran forward into the corridor.

I heard an almighty crash as the beast smashed its way into the school. It was inside and it was right on my tail. I found a staircase and bounded up it three steps at a time. As the staircase turned, I caught sight of the beast not far behind. The claws on its feet scratched and gouged the hardwood floor. It growled and snarled as it followed my scent.

I reached the second floor and burst into a classroom. I ran to the back and crawled under a desk. I hoped it hadn't seen me. I tried to control my breathing, but my chest heaved. I couldn't run any more.

The beast sniffed at the door. I looked around me and realised I'd trapped myself in a corner. There was no way out. The werewolf pushed the door open with its snout and slowly entered the room.

I hunkered down under the desk and held my breath. The beast moved slowly but the smell of its matted fur instantly filled the room. A desk screeched across the floor as the beast brushed past. It was getting closer. It was almost at the back row of desks. I had nowhere to go, and soon I'd have nowhere to hide. The windows were shut and the beast was between me and the door.

It sniffed the air. Two more seconds and it would be on me. It padded forward. I was out of ideas, but then the door crashed open again.

"Hey, you big dumb dog!" Zaza yelled, waving her arms above her head. "Come on, you smelly mutt! Why don't you pick on someone your own size?"

The werewolf span around and leapt towards the door. Zaza ducked and was gone. I could hear her footsteps disappear into the distance as the beast followed.

Zaza had saved me. Now, it was my turn to save her.

CHAPTER TWENTY-FOUR

I CRAWLED OUT from under the desk and ran towards the door. I could hear the werewolf smashing its way around the school. I had to help Zaza, so I started running towards the destruction.

I jumped over fallen lockers and skipped between broken shards of glass as I followed in the beast's wake. I could hear a commotion up ahead and sprinted to reach Zaza in time. I flew around the corner and… crashed right into Mr Michaels.

"What on earth is going on here!?" he demanded. "I leave you alone for two minutes…"

"WEREWOLF!" I shouted. I couldn't think to explain in more detail. "Werewolf! Zaza!"

Mr Michaels took a step back and looked around. He might think I'm crazy but he couldn't ignore the devastation in the hallway.

"…where?" he said, finally.

I didn't stop to explain. I ran and he followed.

Eventually, I realised I could no longer hear the sound of the werewolf. I'd lost its trail. The path of destruction had doubled back on itself and I couldn't tell which way it had gone. Mr Michaels and I crept slowly along the first floor. No words were exchanged between us. We started opening every classroom door we came across and looking inside for Zaza. I was opening the door to a geography classroom when I saw something out the corner of my eye.

A backpack was peeking out from under a broken bit of wood.

"Is it hers?" Mr Michaels asked.

"Yeah," I said, opening the zip and peering at the books inside. "She must have passed through here. Come on."

We regrouped and picked up the pace again until, suddenly, we heard a noise coming from a nearby science classroom.

"Shhhh!" Mr Michaels hissed.

We crouched down and approached the door. Mr Michaels peered through the window. He paused. The door swung open and Zaza raced out.

She nearly knocked me over as she ran. Mr Michaels and I looked at each other and then ran after her. She burst through the exterior doors and we followed her out into the courtyard.

"Wait! WAIT!" Mr Michaels yelled, breathlessly. "You need to tell me what is going on here."

Zaza stopped and we both turned to face the janitor.

"There's a werewolf," she said, slowly. Calmly. Mr Michaels twitched.

"A werewolf? In the daytime?" he asked.

"I know you won't believe us," Zaza said. "So, I'll show you. I know where it went."

Zaza started walking to the edge of the courtyard.

"It went this way about five minutes ago," she said. "It can't have gone far."

We proceeded slowly, keeping our eyes peeled for any sort of movement. We were headed towards Mr Michaels' supply shed. As we turned the corner, there was a loud roar and a dark shadow launched itself towards us.

"Is this all some kind of sick joke?" Mr Michaels asked as Ellie stood in front of us roaring like a tiger.

CHAPTER TWENTY-FIVE

"THAT'S IT. I'M calling your parents. This joke has gone too far!" Mr Michaels shouted.

He was furious. We tried to explain but it was no use, he'd already started marching off towards reception. As we saw him disappear around the corner, Ellie turned to me.

"What's his problem?" she said, waving her furry arms in his direction.

"We have to go," Zaza said quickly. "We can't wait here. It'll be back."

"What'll be back? What's going on?" Ellie asked.

"That's a good question," I added, turning to Zaza.

"Look," she said. "It wasn't me scaring you. It was the beasts. The werewolves that I told you about!"

"They're …real?" Eliie whispered.

"It happens after school. I've seen them when it gets dark, but never this early, never when the sun is still up. I tried to warn you." Zaza said, her voice wavering.

"It's true," I said, as Ellie looked at me for confirmation.

"We have to get help," Ellie said, realising the gravity of the situation. "We need to find some adults."

"Mr Michaels is the only person I've seen since the bell rang," Zaza said, looking around. "And there's no way he'll listen now."

"Mr Cruft will know what to do," I interjected. Something about the situation made me think of him.

We made our way back into the school. Ellie looked around in shock as she saw what the werewolf had done.

"It's real?" she said. "I mean like, *really* real."

We kept walking up to the second floor and towards Mr Cruft's classroom. The door creaked open. He wasn't there. As we stepped into the dusty room, it was obvious something wasn't right. Tables were on their sides and chairs were scattered across the floor.

"Did you come in here when it was following you?" I asked, turning to Zaza.

"No," she said slowly. "Look at this."

She pointed to the wall. Large scratch marks had been made through all the student's work that was on display.

"It was here," I said.

"And here," Ellie added, looking at Mr Cruft's desk. His paperwork had been shredded into pieces and the wooden surface was splintered and torn.

"So it must've come here sometime before we saw it in the playground?" I asked.

"It must've got Mr Cruft!" Ellie said.

"Or…" Zaza interrupted. "There is another possibility."

Something about her tone made me stop and listen. She spoke quietly but we knew it was serious.

"Maybe…" she continued. "It didn't take Mr Cruft. Maybe it *is* Mr Cruft."

There was an eery silence as Ellie and I processed the information. Was it really possible that Mr Cruft was a werewolf? I looked at his desk again. The deep scratches cut across the surface as if whatever made them was sitting in Mr Cruft's chair.

"I've seen them before." Zaza continued. "From my bedroom window. I see them move in the shadows, but I never see any teachers leave. They must still be here in some form." As Ellie went to speak, we heard a noise. A smash of glass.

"It's back!" Zaza hissed.

CHAPTER TWENTY-SIX

"IT'S BENEATH US," I said. "Ground floor."

We heard a bang.

"We need to move," Zaza said.

We rushed to the door as quickly as we could. Ellie tugged at the fur on her face and arms and chucked it to the floor as she ran.

"Quiet!" I whispered. "If it hears us, we're doomed."

We left the classroom and turned left along the deserted corridor. We had to get past the stairwell without the werewolf hearing us. I went first and signalled for the others to follow. I crouched down low and moved slowly along the wall. The entrance to the stairwell came and went. We'd passed the first test.

"There's another exit further up this way," Zaza whispered, gesturing further along the corridor.

We crept forward as the banging from below continued. The beast was moving along the floor directly beneath us.

“Is it following us? It didn’t see us, did it?” Ellie said.

“I think it can smell us,” I replied, thinking of how much Mr Michaels’ dog Skungus likes to sniff at our clothes.

“Stop chatting,” Zaza said. “We need to keep moving or we’ll all be dog food.”

Zaza was right, we had to keep going. We proceeded along the corridor. Moving slowly, we tried not to make a sound. I placed each foot down gently and we edged closer to our goal.

The beast went quiet.

We froze.

If it heard us now, there’d be no escape. We held our breath and waited. Finally, it moved again. The sound of its claws scraping on the walls echoed around the school. I gestured to the others and we moved forward. As we rounded the corner, we saw the stairwell at the end of the hall.

“That’s our way out,” I said.

We moved forward again. With the exit so close, we picked up the pace. We could still hear the beast somewhere below, but it seemed farther away now. We moved quicker, almost running. The sound of the beast died down completely as we reached the stairs.

“I think it’s gone,” I said, with a smile.

“Let’s leave, quick!” Ellie said, grabbing the handrail and heading downstairs.

“Something’s not right,” Zaza said, waiting at the top.

“What do you mean? Come on!” I said, bounding after Ellie.

“It’s too quiet,” Zaza said. “It’s not normal.”

“You’re being paranoid! It’s gone!” I shouted back.

I reached the bottom of the stairs and bumped straight into Ellie. She was standing dead still, staring ahead. I followed her eye-line and saw it. Standing in front of us, its bright eyes shining in the dingy hallway, was the towering figure of a fully grown werewolf.

CHAPTER TWENTY-SEVEN

IT ROARED. WE screamed. The combined noise made the walls shake and the dust jump. We turned and ran, taking the stairs three at a time. The werewolf leapt after us. Its jaws snapped at our ankles but we didn't look back. We kept running, shouting the whole time for Zaza to go too.

The beast was right behind us as we reached the top of the stairs and saw Zaza's terrified face turn and flee. We followed her into the corridor.

"This way!" she screamed.

We bolted through the school with the werewolf hot on our heels. We flew past classrooms, vaulted fallen lockers and skipped frantically over broken glass. The beast never let up. It was still right behind us, smashing through the things we were jumping over.

We doubled back on ourselves and headed for the exit. We turned a corner and saw the double doors a second before bursting through them and falling into the daylight beyond. We crashed to the floor on top of each other and scrambled madly to our feet before the werewolf could catch us.

The doors blew off their hinges and flew across the courtyard. The beast landed with a thud and skidded to a stop. It looked up in time to see us sprinting towards reception. The doors to the main office were bigger and stronger than anywhere else in the school. If we'd be safe anywhere, it would be there.

We heard another inhuman growl as the werewolf started chasing us again. In the open ground, we were no match for its incredible speed. I looked over my shoulder and saw it running on all fours. Spit and snot whipped around its nose and mouth. Its teeth were bared and its eyes focussed.

The gap between us closed quickly but we managed to reach reception just in time. We hurried inside and braced ourselves against the door as the beast slammed against the outside. The hinges rattled and the doors buckled but they stayed shut.

The beast backed off and sniffed at the air. I grabbed one end of a sofa and dragged it in front of the doors. Once the first one was in place, Zaza and Ellie helped me pull another one over to add to the barricade. Soon, we had three sofas, a coffee table and a potted plant stacked solidly between us and the werewolf.

We looked around us and took stock of our surroundings. There was only one other entrance but the werewolf would have to go around the whole building to get to us there.

"We need to get out of here," Ellie said, finally catching her breath.

“And go where?” Zaza replied. “The path from that door goes all the way round to the courtyard where that mutt is waiting for us.”

She was right. We were trapped.

I peered out the barricaded doors at the beast as it prowled back and forth, waiting for its dinner. This was the first time I’d been able to get a good look at it. It was as huge as it was ugly. The fur on its chest was matted from all the drool that had dripped down onto it. Its limbs were long and bony. It moved clumsily back and forth like it wasn’t used to its own body, but there was a glint in its eyes that looked like it knew what I was thinking. It stared straight back at me as I took it all in.

“What are we going to do?” Ellie asked.

I had no answer. I looked around the room for inspiration but nothing came. The beast was outside and we were inside. We were safe for now, but our barricade wouldn’t last long. It was us versus the werewolf. The school was deserted.

Or so we thought.

CHAPTER TWENTY-EIGHT

THE WEREWOLF APPROACHED the door. It sniffed at the hinges and retreated a few paces.

"Something's spooked it," Zaza said. "It's confused."

"What did it smell?" Ellie asked.

"It smelled us," my dad said.

We span round to see Mum and Dad coming in the back doors with Mr Michaels and Skungus. We ran to our parents and jumped into their arms.

"I'm so sorry," Dad said. "We should've told you."

"Should have told them what?" Zaza said.

Everyone turned to face her.

"This is Zaza," I said. "A friend from class."

"What should you have told them?" she repeated, not caring for the introductions.

"I should've told them why we moved here. I should've told them what my job is," he sighed.

Mr Michaels checked the barricade.

"I work," my dad continued, "in the animal research department. Only, the animals we research aren't …normal."

"You knew this was here?" Ellie said, tears welling in her eyes.

"No!" Mum replied. "We had no idea it was in the school until Mr Michaels rang us and told us what had happened."

"They're normally very solitary creatures," Dad reasoned. "We assumed they'd stay out in the sticks where there are no people. That's where I've been going every day. That's where they *should've* been."

"So, how do we fix it?" I said.

My dad looked at me and smiled.

"That's the spirit, Son. The thing with werewolves is they are very stupid beasts. The key to defeating them is to make them so confused they don't know what's happening. We need to think of some way of baffling it. Once it's flustered, it'll become dazed and easy to manipulate. Then we can lead it somewhere safe until morning comes."

"Oh, no problem," Zaza said. "We'll just give it my maths homework, then. Easy."

"This is serious," Ellie replied. "We need to lead it somewhere that'll make it confused."

"That's just it!" I said, suddenly. "I know exactly what to do!"

CHAPTER TWENTY-NINE

"THE WHIRLYBIRD!" I shouted. "It confused the hell out of me."

Zaza laughed, clearly remembering the P.E. lesson where I'd spent most of the time laying face-first in mud.

"He's right, it did," she said with a grin. "But, we might need something a bit more difficult to confuse animals."

"*Har har*," I said, sarcastically. "Let's go. We'll split into two groups and meet back up at the climbing frame. That *thing* won't know who to follow and we'll be fine until we get there."

"And then what?" Ellie asked.

I felt five sets of eyes staring at me.

"Then," I said. "We play."

We left through the back door and crept around to the front of the school. When the werewolf saw us it let out a blood-curdling, teeth-rattling roar. Ellie jumped and clung onto my arm.

"Run!" I shouted.

We split into two groups and took off in different directions. Mr Michaels, Skungus and my parents arched round to the left while I went with Ellie and Zaza to the right. I hoped the beast would follow me instead of Mum and Dad as we sprinted through the playground. When I looked back, I was relieved to see it had.

My relief quickly turned to fear as the werewolf bounded across the school on all fours. Its claws scuffed the concrete and bits of drool flew backwards from its mouth as it moved. We had a good head start but it was gaining fast.

We reached the climbing frame just in time and jumped hastily onto the swinging benches. The werewolf skidded to a halt as we leapt from swing to swing, carefully avoiding the ones that were rigged to fail. Its eyes darted back and forth, not knowing where to look.

Luckily, it was still distracted when the others arrived. They sprinted past the beast and leapt across the void to join us on the swings. Mr Michaels arrived last with Skungus in his arms like an over-sized baby. I screamed instructions to them as they climbed onto the planks and successfully avoided the booby-trapped steps.

The werewolf leapt forward and crashed onto the first plank. It scrambled madly to keep its footing as the swing rocked violently back and forth. Finally, it settled enough for the beast to move forward again. Locking us in its sights, it sprung through the air and landed face-first into the mud below. It had fallen for the same trick I had. The plank it landed on gave way beneath its feet and the beast crumpled into a pile on the floor.

It raised its head and regained its senses.

"I think we've angered it!" Ellie said.

It shook its entire body and its ruffled fur settled down back into place as bits of mud were propelled across the playground. It clearly decided the swinging planks weren't worth the effort. It lifted one paw out of the claggy mud and, slowly but surely, started moving towards us again. Walking through the mud would slow the beast down, but it wouldn't stop it.

I reached the doors and waited for the beast to be looking at me before I burst through the first one. I wasted no time and ran through the doors in the exact order that was drummed into me during our fateful P.E. lesson. Through a crack in the next door, I saw the beast cock its head to the side.

Ellie followed, then Zaza, then the others in turn with the adults following the kids through the correct doors. Soon, we were all through the doors and the beast had reached the end of the muddy pit. It bowed low on its hind legs and sprung forward …straight into a rock-solid door-frame. It bounced backwards and skidded into the mud. For a second, it was dazed. It looked up at the doors and cocked its head to the side. It was confused but still angry.

The snarling beast approached the doors again. It could smell our fear on the far side. It nudged the second door with its nose. It swung gently open. The beast proceeded through the first line with a renewed swagger.

It drew itself up to its full height before bursting into a low sprint. Its razor-sharp teeth glistened in the fading sunlight as it reached the second row of doors. It surged forward and slammed into another locked door.

It sat down again, its head turning from side to side. It didn't understand. It could smell us, even hear us on the other side of the doors. It saw us move through them but it couldn't figure out what was happening.

Its teeth were no longer bared and it sat gently back on its haunches. The confusion was overwhelming it. It was becoming a lapdog.

"It's working!" I whispered.

I looked at Ellie expecting her to share my excitement, but her eyes were wide and sweat dripped from her brow. She was terrified.

I followed her eye-line and saw why.

CHAPTER THIRTY

THREE MORE WEREWOLVES were approaching. Their large, clumsy bodies dragged their way across the playground and approached the climbing frame.

"Is that one wearing ...shorts?" Zaza whispered, as we all hunched on various swinging doors.

I peered through a gap and saw one of the beasts did, in fact, have a pair of green gym shorts curled tightly around one leg.

"They're Mrs Harrison's shorts!" Mr Michaels said, his voice cracking. "Oh god, they've eaten her!"

"I don't think they've eaten her," I said, looking at the werewolf's long blonde fur. "I think it *is* her." The beasts gathered together. The original creature's trance seemed to be broken by the arrival of the others.

"Look," Dad said, "The one with the shorts isn't bothered by this at all!"

The blonde werewolf sniffed the Whirlybird and leapt gracefully onto the first plank. Then, without hesitation, it jumped to the next. And then the next. It proceeded effortlessly across all the planks in the correct order, avoiding every false step.

"Did you say that was a teacher?" Dad continued. "What, exactly, did it teach?"

"P.E." I said, softly. "She built this climbing frame…"

My dad paused, taking in the information. Then, suddenly, he screamed.

"RUN!"

We burst from the climbing frame and scattered in all directions. I ran as hard as I could back towards the school. The werewolves howled together and gave chase. I looked behind me and saw one of them on my tail. It growled and choked on its own phlegm as it ate up the ground between us.

I rushed around the corner as the beast jumped towards me. Its razor-sharp claws grazed my back as I managed to hurl myself away from its grasp just in time. It flew past and slid into a wall.

In the distance, I saw Mum and Dad beckoning me towards reception. They were already inside and preparing a barricade. I glanced backwards. The werewolf had jumped to its feet, howled to the sky and set off to hunt me down again.

I ran as fast as I could towards the safety of reception. I could hear every snort and grunt from the animal behind me. Snot and spit flailing, it hauled its huge body forwards.

My bicycle races against Ellie had paid off, I ran fast and maintained my speed. I was just a few metres from the door when the beast made a desperate lung at my back. I could feel the wind press against me as the beast flew through the air with its claws drawn.

I jumped at the same time and just managed to avoid its snapping jaws. I skidded past my screaming parents and heard the werewolf slaw into the doors they'd closed behind me. I jumped up and helped add material to the barricade as all four werewolves started to fling themselves at the doors.

"We're safe for now, but it won't last long," my dad said, turning to face us.

"What happened back there? Why did you tell us to run? It was working! The plan was working!" Zaza said, desperately.

"It wasn't working," Dad replied calmly. "The wolf with the shorts, you said that was the teacher who designed the climbing frame?"

"Yeah, so what?"

"So, they can sometimes retain information from their other lives. She clearly knew how the swings worked. She designed them!"

"She walked right past them," Ellie said.

"She would've walked straight to us and eaten us all alive, Skungus included," Dad said, finally.

Nobody spoke for a second as we all processed what had just happened. Three beasts continued to throw themselves at the barricade. The fourth had made its way around the back and scratched feverishly at the other set of doors.

We were trapped.

CHAPTER THIRTY-ONE

THE BEASTS WERE nearly inside. The glass cracked and the brickwork crumbled. Ellie and Zaza huddled together in the corner. Dad was comforting Mum to the side. Mr Michaels was hugging Skungus.

Suddenly, I had an idea. Seeing Mr Michaels and his dog made me remember something. It was crazy, but it might just work…

"Give me the whistle!" I shouted.

Mr Michaels looked at me blankly.

"The dog whistle! That you use with Skungus!" I added.

He reached into his pocket and held out the rusty tin whistle. Skungus fixed his eyes on it. The werewolves tore at the barrier. A few more seconds and they'd be inside,

"Quick!" I screamed as the last of the barrier fell to the floor.

The beasts burst through the door with a howl. Mr Michaels threw the whistle. It looped up high but I plucked it out of the air and blew hard.

The werewolves slowed.

Spit dripped from their fangs as they came straight towards me. I raised the whistle to my lips again and blew two sharp bursts.

The beasts dropped to the floor and sat to attention.

Three more toots and they rolled over.

"They're like puppies…" Ellie said, smiling brightly again.

"Fascinating. Simply, fascinating," Dad muttered.

"Make them do tricks!" Zaza added.

I walked from left to right and the beasts watched me intently, waiting for instructions.

"Just like Skungus!" I said, triumphantly.

I handed the whistle to Mr Michaels and the werewolves followed it, waiting for the next instruction.

"I'll keep them safe until morning," he said. "They can use some of Skungus's old chew toys."

I felt a tug at my arm and turned to see Ellie coming in for a hug.

"Is it really over?" she asked, pulling back.

"It's really over," I said.

That evening, Zaza came over for a BBQ in the garden with the whole family. We filled ourselves up on burgers and hotdogs and roast salmon. We played games, told jokes and laughed until we cried. Everything was perfect until the football landed in Mr Ramsey's garden.

I clambered over some daffodils and hoisted myself up to peer over the rickety brown fence.

"Sorry, Mr Ramsey!" I yelled, to the figure in the garden. "Can we have our ball back please?"

Mr Ramsey stopped and stared into the distance. He was facing away from me, but I'm sure he heard.

"Mr Ramsey?" I repeated.

He bent down low and picked up the football. Slowly, he turned to face me, his bright red eyes peering into my soul.

"Dad!" I screamed. "Get the whistle. QUICK!"

More SCARETOWN books available now.

Cassie and Daniel like nothing more than to explore new places during the summer holidays. However, there is one place they don't go. Dead Man's Woods. The creepy forest near their house is strictly out of bounds, until one day they're forced to enter its dark interior. Now, Cassie and Daniel must fight to escape what lurks amongst the ancient trees.

DEAD MAN'S WOODS is as fun as it is horrifying. Anyone brave enough to pick it up is in for the thrill of a lifetime.

AVAILABLE TO BUY NOW ON AMAZON OR READ FOR FREE ON KINDLE UNLIMITED.

More SCARETOWN books available now.

Theo and Eddie Jensen think they've found the perfect game to play after school, but things change when they are tricked by a teacher and become stuck in the VR world. Now, they must hurry to find a way back to real life before the switch is made permanent and they're trapped in virtual reality forever.

VR NIGHTMARE is a riot of extreme fun and awesome adventure packed from start to finish with screams, laughs and gasps.

AVAILABLE TO BUY NOW ON AMAZON OR READ FOR FREE ON KINDLE UNLIMITED.

DEAD MAN'S WOODS

1.

We'd been living in our new neighbourhood for two months before I plucked up the courage to enter Dead Man's Woods. The school holidays had started and the summer heat made the house unbearable. Sweat dripped from my face as I chucked my puzzle book to the side and hauled myself towards the front door.

"Cassie!" Arj shouted when I opened it. He stood on the doorstep with a stupid grin.

"What is it, Arj?" I said, feeling a wave of humid air slap me across the face.

"Come with me, I've got something to show you."

"But, it's so hot. I just want to stay inside and melt," I said, wiping my brow again.

"Come on!" he pleaded. "You'll like it, I promise."

Arj was the only person I'd spoken to in my new school. He wasn't the coolest or smartest kid in class, but he was always kind and made me feel welcome when everything was scary and new. On my first day, he made space at his desk and invited me to join him. We'd hung out at every break time since.

"OK," I said, "But it better be worth it!"

I slipped into my trainers but, just as I was stepping out the door, I heard a booming voice shouting from the other room.

"WHERE DO YOU THINK YOU'RE GOING, YOUNG LADY?" my mum called.

"Out!" I said, simply.

"Not without your little brother, you're not,' she said, more calmly. "Look at him, he needs a good airing."

I peeked back through the door to see my brother Daniel slouched on the sofa, playing on his phone.

"Come on, get up!" Mum said, grabbing him by the arm and hoisting him into the air. "It'll do you good to get out the house for a bit."

"But, Mum!" Daniel moaned, "I don't wanna hang out with Cassie and her boyfriend!"

"Arj isn't my boyfriend!" I said sharply. I could feel the blood rushing to my cheeks.

"Nonsense," Mum continued. "She's your sister. You'll have fun together. This isn't a discussion. And while you're at it, you can take Smoke for a walk."

Smoke was our dog. A 3-year-old, jet-black Doberman that would scare the life out of almost everyone who saw her but, in reality, was the softest, most cuddly puppy-dog you could ever meet. Mum ushered us out the door and, together with Arj, we stumbled forward into the street.

"You can hang out with us, but don't be annoying!" I said, turning to face Daniel. He shrugged and looked down at his phone again.

"Hi, Daniel!" Arj said with a smile. "Hi, Smoke!"

Smoke wagged her stumpy tail enthusiastically. Daniel grunted.

"That means hello in Daniel-speak," I said.

"I didn't know you were bilingual," Arj said, before giggling to himself as if he had said something funny. I smiled and nodded.

"What was it you wanted to show me, anyway?"

"You're gonna love it!" Arj said as we started walking. Daniel trailed along behind, face down, engrossed in his phone.

"Where is it?" I asked. "What is it?"

"Up there," Arj replied with a nod that made me stop in my tracks.

"In …Dead Man's Woods?" I asked, trying to sound casual. I tugged at my t-shirt to let the air flow more freely. The sun was beating down and the air was still.

I lifted my hand to shield my eyes. Through a gap in a row of houses, we could see a line of tall, dark green trees. Dead Man's Woods, as it was known to all the kids at school, was a dense and overgrown area on the very edge of town. Nobody had ever ventured into Dead Man's Woods. One time, when a football landed in the trees, the players decided to buy a new one rather than go into the spooky undergrowth.

"We're going to Dead Man's Woods!?" Daniel said, looking up from his phone for the first time.

"No, of course not! It's just next to it. We won't go in, I promise!" Arj replied, as we entered an alleyway between two sets of houses.

It wasn't until too late that I realised, some promises are made to be broken.

DEAD MAN'S WOODS is available now. Read the whole book for free on Kindle Unlimited or purchase online. Visit www.scaretownbooks.com for more information.

Join the conversation at www.twitter.com/scaretownbooks

Printed in Great Britain
by Amazon